Indigo and Moonlight Gold

**Written and
Illustrated
by
Jan Spivey Gilchrist**

Published for Black Butterfly Children's Books
by Writers and Readers Publishing, Inc.
P.O. Box 461, Village Station
New York, NY 10014
c/o Airlift Book Company
26 Eden Grove
London N7 8EF
England

Library of Congress Cataloging Card Number 92-053805
ISBN 0-86316-210-X
10 9 8 7 6 5 4 3 2 1

Illustrations in oils on canvas.

For Marie Brown, Eloise Greenfield and Glenn Thompson for your faith in me. Special thanks to Sheena Renee Woodcox.

Autrie got up from the sofa where she had sat next to her mother.

"Can I go out on the porch now, Mama?" Autrie whispered so as not to awaken her brothers and sisters and Daddy sleeping in their rooms.

On these special nights when everyone had turned in early and she and Mama had stayed up and talked and laughed quietly until they each wanted to be alone, and yet together, Autrie would ask to go out on the porch, while Mama watched from the window.

Mama answered yes and Autrie walked slowly toward the door. She could see the night flowing in through the window. Its colors were indigo and moonlight gold. The night filled the room and painted Mama in its colors.

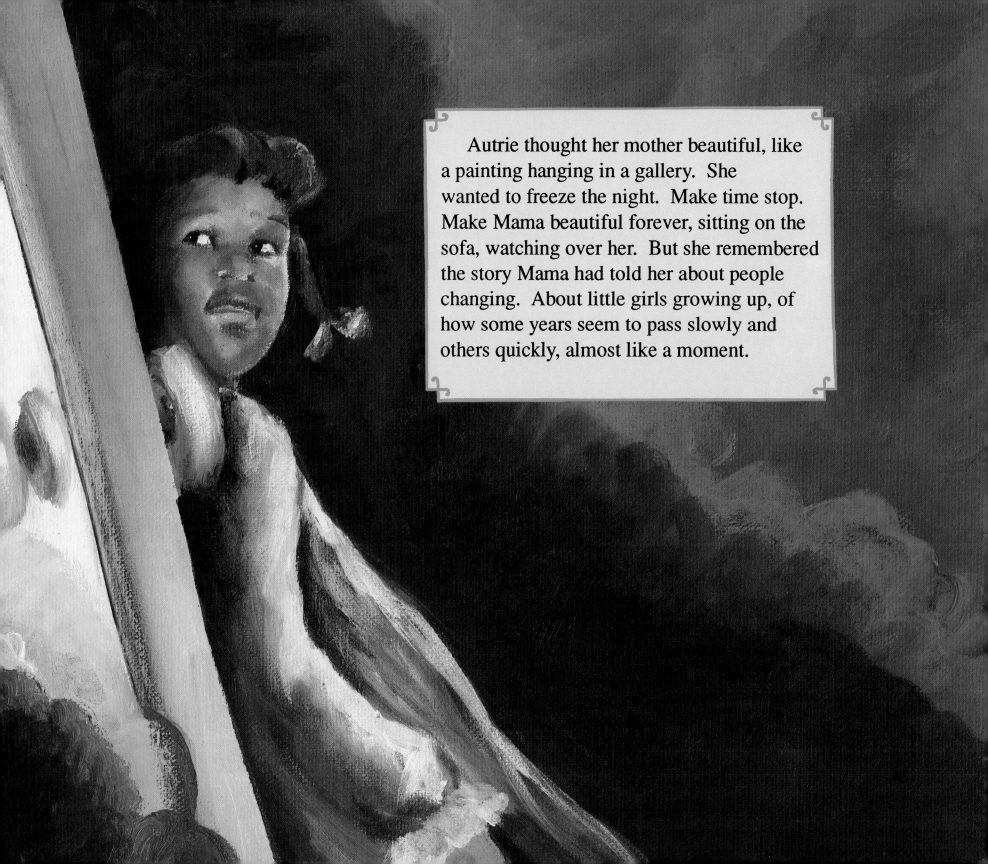

Autrie thought her mother beautiful, like a painting hanging in a gallery. She wanted to freeze the night. Make time stop. Make Mama beautiful forever, sitting on the sofa, watching over her. But she remembered the story Mama had told her about people changing. About little girls growing up, of how some years seem to pass slowly and others quickly, almost like a moment.

She turned away from the painting of Mama and walked out onto the porch. The air was warm, the stars hung low and dangled all around her. She wanted to keep the stars forever.

She lifted her arms, commanding the sky to freeze the scene, but then she dropped them. She knew that clouds must sometimes come and hide the stars.

Autrie closed her eyes. A breeze blew past, encircling her gown. She thought the breeze a mahogany brown blanket, the color of her Mama's eyes. She tried to move deeper inside it and make a place where she could stay forever.

She opened her eyes, allowing the blanket to blow past. She knew the breeze would one day blow cold and winters would come. But she'd be strong against them. Mama would not need to keep her warm.

Getting tired, Autrie rested, lying down,
her back against the cool wood of the porch.
She looked around at Green Street.

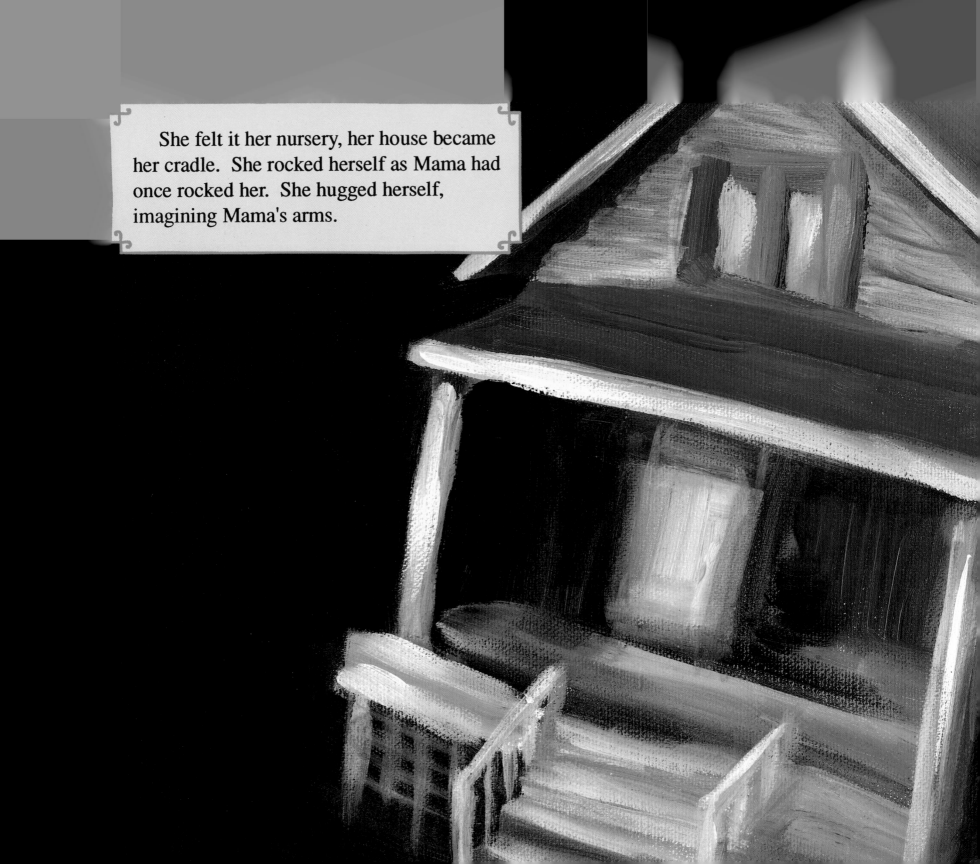

She felt it her nursery, her house became
her cradle. She rocked herself as Mama had
once rocked her. She hugged herself,
imagining Mama's arms.

She could feel her mother's eyes now,
strong on her, and turned to see her shape
in the window.

Autrie raised herself to look closer. She could no longer see her mother's eyes. She blinked and looked again. The shape was gone.

She got up and walked toward the door.

Autrie knew she could not freeze the night or keep the neighborhood wrapped around her. She knew that Mamas don't sit and watch forever. That nights turn to days, starry nights to cloudy ones, and winds blow cold.

And little girls sometimes become Mamas

who sit and watch their children dream on nights of indigo and moonlight gold.